The Man Who Loved Violins

By **Suzanne Wallace**

Illustrations by: **Alexis Jover**

To order additional copies of this book, contact:
Xlibris Corporation
1-888-795-4274
www.Xlibris.com
Orders@Xlibris.com

Dedication

This book is dedicated to Lawrence and Pauline for first putting the music in my heart; and my children and grandchildren for keeping it playing.

There once was a man who loved violins,
He would buy them and put them away,
He could polish them and care for them completely,
But try as he might, he could not play.

He knew there was music
within them,
He knew because he
could hear it in his heart,
But he could not pluck
the strings, and he could
not use the bow,
And he could not tell the
notes apart.

The man would shop in every store
When he traveled far and wide,
But violins were the only souvenirs he bought
In his visits to the countryside.

The violins were soon filling
his every closet,
And they were occupying
every cranny and nook.
They were piled high on the
shelves and on the cupboards,
They were everywhere that
you would look.

You could see them through
his windows,
You could see them through
his door,
And pretty soon his violins
Completely covered the man's
floor.

He longed to hear the music
of the violins,
He dreamed of the songs they
played,
But unfortunately since he
could not make that music,
Wherever the violins were
placed, they just stayed.

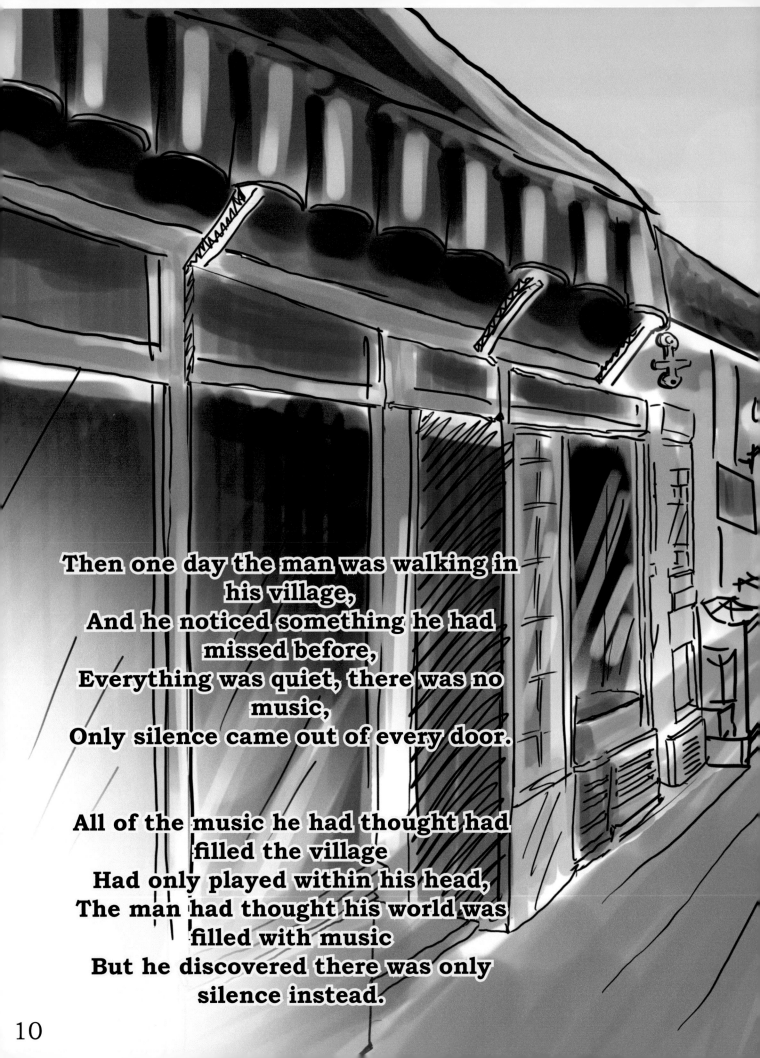

Then one day the man was walking in
his village,
And he noticed something he had
missed before,
Everything was quiet, there was no
music,
Only silence came out of every door.

All of the music he had thought had
filled the village
Had only played within his head,
The man had thought his world was
filled with music
But he discovered there was only
silence instead.

He looked about and people were quite gloomy,
No one had a kind word or a smile,
Each one went straight about his business,
Looking serious and proper all the while.

Now the man knew that his house was filled
with music,
But he needed someone to make it play,
And so he decided he would change things,
And he would begin that very day.

15

He found a little boy who was sad and lonely,
And the man gave him a violin for a gift,
That made the little boy happy
And gave his spirits a lift.

The man gave violins to children in a hospital,
He thought it might make them feel well,
And the doctors said the music made a difference
When they checked on the children, they could tell.

The man gave violins to the children in the school,
And a teacher taught them how to play,
Everyone was grateful for his gift,
For music filled the halls from that very day.

For every violin he gave away, he found another,
It was quite a remarkable thing,
And every time the man walked around the village,
Another violin to a child he would bring.

Then an amazing thing began to happen,
In every home and up and down the street,
Music began to fill the air of the village,
And people smiled as they heard the music's beat.

Other people looked for long forgotten instruments
Which they now began to play,
And in rediscovering their own delight in music,
The village had awakened to a new and happy day.

17

No longer was anyone gloomy,
No longer were the people of the village sad,
For the man had given away his treasure,
And a gift of music is what the village now had.

The children shared their music in the park
Where they played for everyone who came to hear,
And they played for those who could not leave
their homes,
Their violin music was a gift that brought great
cheer.

People heard about the wonderful music of the village,
And they traveled there from miles around.
They began a yearly violin festival,
For no one could resist that lovely sound.

Now the man's house had, in the giving, become quite empty
The cupboards and the shelves were almost bare,
But when he looked around to see what was left,
He found a lovely violin upon a chair.

And then the man who had
brought music to his village,
And with his gifts had done
it in a special way,
Picked up the final violin
that was left there,
And suddenly he began to
play.

23

Printed in the United States
by Baker & Taylor Publisher Services